MID-CONTINENT PUBLIC LIBRARY - BRO
15616 E. 24 HWY.
INDEPENDENCE, MO 64050

3 0000 13444850 9

WITHDRAWN
FROM THE RECORDS OF THE
MID-CONTINENT PUBLIC LIBRARY

D1402310

Sign for
Woodneath
Please

SHARE WITH BROTHER

Happy Readings

SHARE WITH

BROTHER

By Steven L. Layne   Pictures by Ard Hoyt

PELICAN PUBLISHING COMPANY

GRETNA 2011

To Tory and Greg, who are just like brothers to me. —Steve

To my friend Steve, for his inspirations one and all. —Ard

Copyright © 2011
By Steven L. Layne

Pictures copyright © 2011
By Ard Hoyt
All rights reserved

The word "Pelican" and the depiction of a pelican are trademarks of Pelican Publishing Company, Inc., and are registered in the U.S. Patent and Trademark Office.

ISBN: 9781589808607

Printed in Singapore
Published by Pelican Publishing Company, Inc.
1000 Burmaster Street, Gretna, Louisiana 70053

Since the day my baby brother came home, I've been waiting for him to grow a little bit. Mommy and Daddy promised he'd be fun when he was older, and Nana told me I'd be lucky to have a brother to play with.

Nobody said anything about *sharing* though.

And **sharing with brother**
is not as easy as everyone thinks.

Sometimes I'm playing animal safari with my friends, and there isn't a mask for brother.

So Mommy borrows *my* mask to give to brother, and he giggles when he puts it on. She fixes the mask so he can see me.

"Share with brother
        and someday brother
                will share with you."

All my friends laugh when brother makes animal sounds, but *I* don't think brother's so funny.

When Nana comes to visit, she always makes a sweet treat while brother takes his nap.

Sometimes, though, he wakes up early . . .

and Nana tells me to give
half the treat to him.

She gives us both a smoochy kiss.
"Share with brother
      and someday brother
            will share with you."

Nana calls brother adorable when he pretends his sweet treat is an airplane, but *I* don't think brother's so cute.

Everywhere we go, everybody tells me to share with brother.

Well, I don't want to!

Our babysitter Muffy said it passing out the crayons

and our neighbor Mrs. Wilson said it tossing out the jacks.

But then when Uncle Lester said it at *my* birthday party, I tossed the gift across the room and said,

"You take it back!"

I always help with the lights when Daddy puts up the Christmas tree. Yesterday, though, brother wanted to help so he grabbed and pulled on *my* string of lights.

I yanked them hard and told him,

**"Go play with your
carrot people!"**

But Daddy gave brother his own string of lights, then lit them up.

"Share with brother and someday brother will share with you."

Daddy said brother was really clever when he pointed to a light that wasn't shining. Well, *I* don't think brother's so smart, and this time I said so! I pulled brother's plug. Daddy sent me to my room.

Today, brother's been in bed since he's not feeling well. Mommy says he needs to be alone. But one thing I know is that sick people need visitors, and no one was coming to visit with brother.

So *I* tippy-toed in.

Brother cheered up right away!

I put my mask on brother, and he growled and made me laugh. I gave him half my ice cream, and we shivered while we ate. I strung some lights around his bed, and he lit up like Christmas!

When I read *our* favorite book out loud, brother fell asleep.

Guess what? Everyone was right.
Sharing *is* easier than I thought.

I shared with brother . . .

and brother shared with me.